written and illustrated by

HELME HEINE

Mr. Miller The Dog

A MARGARET K. McELDERRY BOOK

Atheneum   1980   *New York*

Library of Congress catalog card number: 80-81298   ISBN 0-689-50174-9
Copyright © 1979 by Friedrich W. Heye Verlag GmbH, München-Hamburg
Translation copyright © 1980 by Atheneum Publishers and J. M. Dent & Sons, Ltd.

Every morning, when Mr. Miller came home from work, his dog Murphy met him at the door.

"Murphy, I'm dog tired. Please bring me my slippers."

"Right away," Murphy growled, knowing that he would get nothing to eat until his master had his slippers.

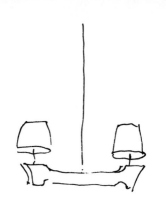

Then Mr. Miller set the table. Murphy was happy.
He knew he would be given something nice to eat.

"Does it taste good, Murphy?"
"Mmm."
"Don't eat so fast! You always finish before I do.
You'll make yourself sick."

After that Mr. Miller read the morning paper for a while.

Before going to sleep, Mr. Miller would tell Murphy what had happened the night before. Mr. Miller was a night watchman.

So the days, weeks, months and years went by. Each morning was very like the one before.

The two of them had grown so used to each other

that Murphy began to look more and more like

Mr. Miller, and Mr. Miller began to look more and more like Murphy.

Perhaps this happened because they lived together,
or perhaps because they envied each other's lives.

Murphy hated waiting alone in the house while Mr. Miller went out to work.

More and more, Mr. Miller thought about the old saying, "It's a dog's life!" Often he would say to Murphy, "Murphy, in my next life, I'd *like* to be a dog—Mr. Miller's dog if possible."

Then they would both laugh

and go back to whatever they were doing.

One evening, Murphy growled, "Listen, Mr. Miller. Why can't we change places? You stay here and I'll take your job as the night watchman."

"Nonsense, Murphy. We can't do that!"

But Murphy did not give up. As the days, weeks, months and years went by, he asked Mr. Miller the same question over and over again.

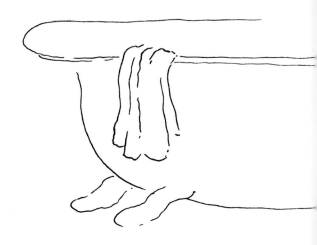

Gradually, as time passed, the idea seemed less and less strange to Mr. Miller, until one morning he said, "Murphy, I have thought this over carefully. Why not?"

That evening, it was Mr. Miller who said goodbye to Murphy at the door. "Do you really think you can manage? If anything goes wrong, we will both lose our job."

"Of course. I will watch like a watchdog. See you in the morning!"

Mr. Miller spent a restless night alone.

At last he heard Murphy climbing the stairs and rattling the keys of the front door.

"Well . . . ? How did it all go?"

"Easier than I thought. Everything went like clockwork. You don't have to worry about a thing."

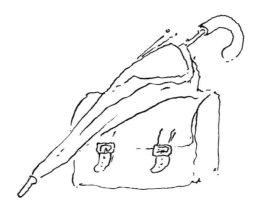

Before going to sleep, they read the morning paper for a while.

So many days, weeks, months and years went by.

One morning, when Murphy came home he said, "Mr. Miller, I'm dog tired. Please bring me my slippers."

"Right away," growled Mr. Miller, for he knew that he would get nothing to eat until Murphy had his slippers.

After that, Murphy set the table. Mr. Miller was happy. He knew he would be given something nice to eat.

"Does it taste good, Mr. Miller?"
"Mmm."
"Don't eat so fast! You always finish before I do.
You'll make yourself sick!"

Before going to bed, Murphy read the morning paper for a while and told Mr. Miller what had happened the night before.

Murphy was a night watchman.